Logan

I am very excited to meet you. You are very blessed to have such a loving family. I wish nothing but but wonderful things for you. Welcome to The World!

Love.
Dana G.

# Big Bird's
# BABY BOOK

## By Michaela Muntean
## Illustrated by Tom Brannon

### Featuring Jim Henson's Sesame Street Muppets

 **A GOLDEN BOOK • NEW YORK**

Published by Golden Books Publishing Company, Inc., in cooperation with Children's Television Workshop

A portion of the money you pay for this book goes to Children's Television Workshop.
It is put right back into SESAME STREET and other CTW educational projects. Thanks for helping!

**B**ig Bird and Elmo held the door of
Hooper's Store open for a lady pushing
a baby carriage.

"Thank you," said the lady. "I hope my
baby grows up to be as polite and helpful
as you two."

"May Elmo see the baby?" Elmo asked.

"Of course," the lady answered. "Her name is Frieda."

"Hello, Frieda," Elmo said softly as he peered into the carriage. "Elmo was once as little as you are."

Big Bird bent down to look at Frieda. "I was once that little, too," he said.

Elmo looked up at Big Bird. "Are you sure?" he asked.

"Of course I'm sure," said Big Bird. "My Granny Bird has an album filled with my baby-bird pictures."

"Elmo would like to see them," said Elmo.

"Okay," Big Bird answered. "Let's go."

They waved good-bye to Frieda and her mommy and set off toward Granny Bird's house.

"I'd be happy to show you the album," Granny Bird said when Elmo asked to see it. "I never get tired of looking at pictures of my little Big Bird."

Granny opened the album. "Look at this one," she said with a sigh. "Wasn't he adorable?"

Elmo looked at the picture. Then he looked at Big Bird. "It doesn't look like you at all," said Elmo.

"Just wait," said Big Bird as Granny
turned the page of the album.
In the next picture the egg had cracked in
two, and between the halves of the shell sat
a little yellow bird.

"He was one of the cutest bunch of feathers ever hatched," said Granny Bird, "and so small, I could tuck him under my wing."

Sure enough, the next picture in the album showed Granny's feathery wing wrapped around the newborn bird.

"I didn't stay little for long," said Big Bird. Granny nodded. "You shot up like a weed. We had to keep making you bigger and bigger nests. That's why we decided to call you Big Bird."

"What's that?" Elmo asked, pointing to a pale yellow feather taped to a page of the album.

"One of Big Bird's baby feathers," Granny explained. "It was the first one he shed as his new feathers began to grow in."

"Look," said Big Bird. "Here I am in my high chair!"

"Yes," said Granny. "You sure liked that birdseed baby cereal. You ate it by the truckload!"

"Here you are taking your first steps,"
said Granny Bird. "And what did you do?
You walked right through a mud puddle!"

"Hee, hee," Elmo giggled. "It was into the
birdbath for you, Big Bird!" he said.

"Here's a picture of a very important day," said Big Bird.

"It's a birthday party!" said Elmo.

"Yes," said Granny. "Big Bird used to call them bird-day parties."

"It's important for another reason," added Big Bird.

"It was the day Radar came to live
with me," he explained.

"You wouldn't go anywhere without
that little bear," said Granny.

"On my next birthday, I got my first pair of roller skates!" said Big Bird.

"And then there was no stopping you," said Granny.

"I was the fastest bird on eight wheels,"
Big Bird said proudly.

"Pretty soon you were big enough to help me make birdseed cookies," said Granny. "You always liked to pour while I stirred."

"I still like to do that," said Big Bird. "Only now I don't need to use the stepladder."

"Would you like to help me make a batch of cookies now?" asked Granny.
"Sure!" said Big Bird.

"Big Bird," said Elmo, "once upon a time you really *were* as little as that baby in Hooper's Store."

"But I'm all grown up now," said Big Bird as he poured the batter into the bowl of birdseed and flour.

"You may think you're all grown up," said Granny, "but you'll always be little Big Bird to me."